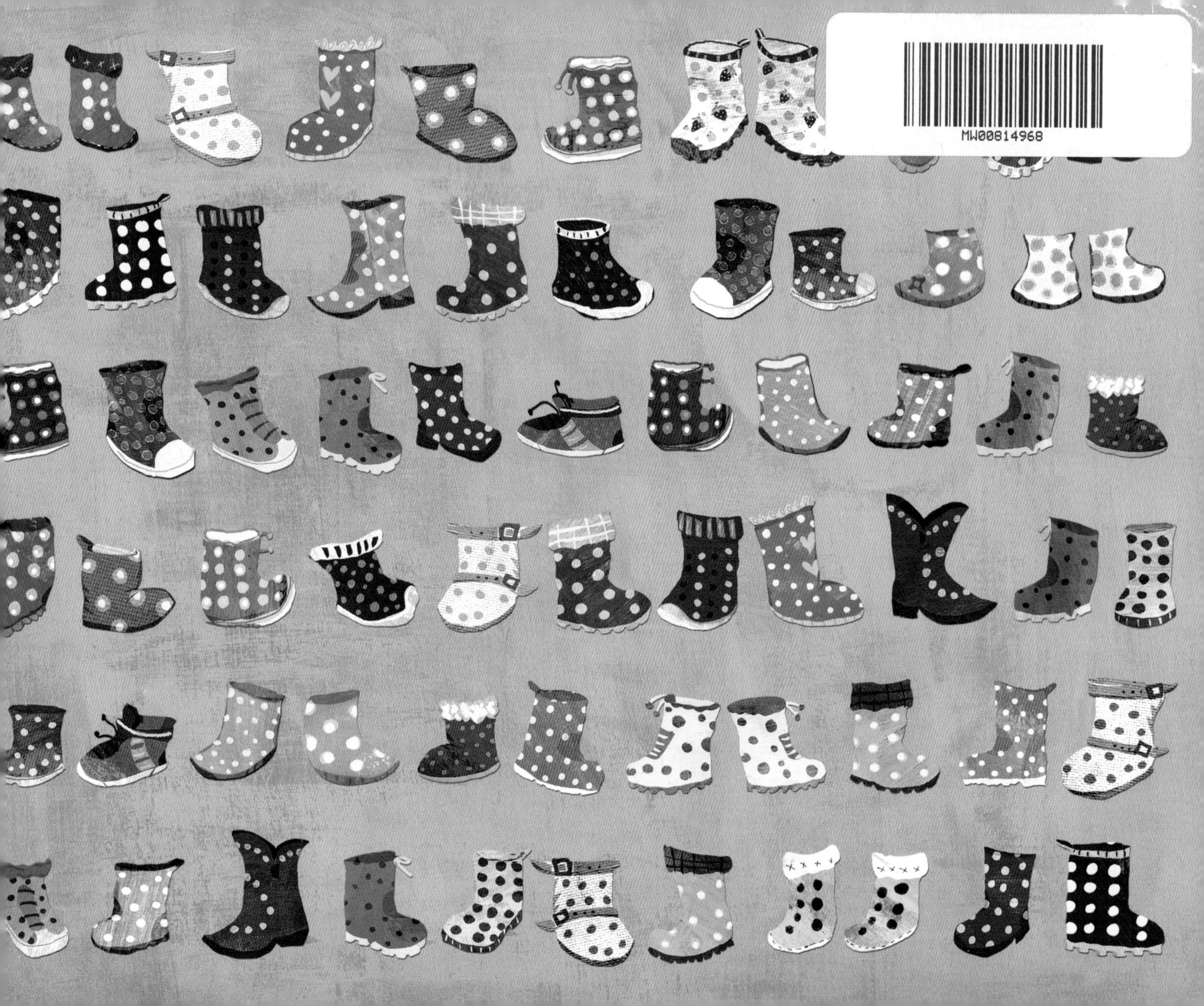
MW00814968

For Nory and Sanche, who are always ooh-la-la! —E.O.B.

To my friend Imke, who's still looking for her perfect pair of boots. —C.E.

Published in the United States by Tricycle Press, an imprint of the
Crown Publishing Group, a division of Random House, Inc., New York.
www.crownpublishing.com
www.tricyclepress.com

Tricycle Press and the Tricycle Press colophon are registered
trademarks of Random House, Inc.

Library of Congress Cataloging-in-Publication Data
Olson-Brown, Ellen, 1967-
Ooh la la polka-dot boots / by Ellen Olson-Brown ; illustrations by Christiane Engel.
p. cm.
Summary: Illustrations and brief rhyming text sing the praises
of polka-dot boots, which add panache to any outfit.
[1. Stories in rhyme. 2. Clothing and dress—Fiction. 3. Boots—Fiction.]
I. Engel, Christiane, ill. II. Title.
PZ8.3.O4988Oo 2010
[E]—dc22

2009007547

ISBN 978-1-58246-287-5

Printed in China

Design by Chloe Rawlins
Typeset in P22 Garamouche and Avenir.
The illustrations in this book were created in acrylics and digital collage.

1 2 3 4 5 6 – 15 14 13 12 11 10

First Edition

Ooh La La Polka-Dot Boots

Written by Ellen Olson-Brown
Illustrated by Christiane Engel

TRICYCLE PRESS
Berkeley

Big Shirts
79
Small Shirts

Short Shirts
Long Shirts
polka-dot boots!

Plain coats

Zany coats

Sun coats
Rainy coats
polka-dot boots!

Hot hats
Cold hats

Silver hats
Gold hats
polka-dot boots!

Ugly pants
Pretty pants

New sweaters

Old sweaters

polka-dot boots!

Over-wear
Underwear

Country pants
City pants
polka-dot boots!

Shy sweaters
Bold sweaters

Whisper-wear
Thunder-wear
polka-dot boots!

Fast duds
Slow duds

Lots of duds
No duds
polka-dot boots!